Karen's

(Baby-Sitters Little Sister #98)

**Other books by
Ann M. Martin**

P.S. Longer Letter Later
(written with Paula Danziger)
Leo the Magnificat
Rachel Parker, Kindergarten Show-off
Eleven Kids, One Summer
Ma and Pa Dracula
Yours Turly, Shirley
Ten Kids, No Pets
With You and Without You
Me and Katie (the Pest)
Stage Fright
Inside Out
Bummer Summer

For older readers:

Missing Since Monday
Just a Summer Romance
Slam Book

THE BABY-SITTERS CLUB series
THE BABY-SITTERS CLUB mysteries
THE KIDS IN MS. COLMAN'S CLASS series
BABY-SITTERS LITTLE SISTER series
(see inside book covers for a complete listing)

Little Sister

Karen's Fishing Trip
Ann M. Martin

Illustrations by Susan Crocca Tang

A
LITTLE **APPLE**
PAPERBACK

SCHOLASTIC INC.
New York Toronto London Auckland Sydney

ISBN 0-590-06596-3

Copyright © 1998 by Ann M. Martin. All rights reserved. Published by Scholastic Inc. BABY-SITTERS LITTLE SISTER and LITTLE APPLE PAPER-BACKS are trademarks and/or registered trademarks of Scholastic Inc.

12 11 10 9 8 7 6 5 4 3 2 1   8 9/9 0 1 2 3/0

Printed in the U.S.A.   40
First Scholastic printing, June 1998

The author gratefully acknowledges
Gabrielle Charbonnet
for her help
with this book.

Summertime at Last!

I was still eating breakfast (a bagel with pineapple cream cheese) when the phone rang. My stepsister, Kristy Thomas, answered it.

"Karen," she said, "it is for you. It is Hannie." She held out the phone.

I gulped and swallowed and leaped for the phone. "Hello?"

"Hi!" said Hannie Papadakis. "Are you dressed? Have you had breakfast? Can I come over? Has Nancy called yet?"

I thought for a second. "Yes, yes, yes, and no," I answered.

"Okay. I will be right over." *Click.* Hannie hung up.

I hung up too. I finished my orange juice. Then I waited for Nancy to call.

My name is Karen Brewer. I am seven years old. It was Monday morning, the first official day of summer vacation. So naturally my two best friends and I wanted to share it.

Soon Nancy Dawes called. She said her mother could drive her to my house. After I hung up the phone, I sat on my front steps to wait for Hannie and Nancy.

I was at my big house. That meant Hannie was just across the street and one house down. Nancy was farther away. She lives next door to my little house. (I will explain all this in awhile. I know it is confusing.)

Ten minutes later Hannie and Nancy had arrived. We all ran into the backyard. We sat down on the grass beneath the big sycamore

2

tree. For awhile we practiced whistling with grass stems.

"Summer, summer, summer," Hannie said happily. She lay on her back and looked up at the sky.

"I know what you mean," said Nancy. She lay down too.

I lay down so that our heads were all touching. We looked at the blue sky and the puffy white clouds that floated overhead. Here is how I felt: If I were any happier, I would just explode.

"There is nothing better than the first day of summer," I said.

"Yup," said Hannie.

Do not get me wrong. I love school. I love my teacher, Ms. Colman. Every day is exciting in Ms. Colman's class. But I also love long summer days, and swimming, and having time for lots of gigundoly great ideas.

"So what should we do this summer?" I asked. "The Three Musketeers need to have the best summer plans ever."

Hannie and Nancy and I call ourselves the Three Musketeers, because we are all for one and one for all.

"Maybe we should not have any definite plans this summer," said Nancy. "Maybe we should let summer *happen* to us."

I did not like that idea. I am a person who feels better knowing what I am going to do. Sometimes I like surprises. But I love to make plans and schedule everything.

"Hmm," I said. That is useful to say when you need more time to think.

"Maybe we could have a *general* list of things to do," said Hannie. "Then we can decide every day."

Nancy and I both thought this was a good idea.

"We have to have a lemonade stand *for sure*," I said.

"We are going to be on Kristy's Krushers again, right?" said Nancy. Kristy's Krushers is my stepsister's softball team.

"Absolutely," said Hannie. "And we have our summer reading list. That means going to the library. And we have to ride our bikes a lot."

"And we have to have tea parties and sleepovers," I said.

"And we have to get ice-cream cones and go to afternoon movies," said Nancy.

Guess what. I felt even happier, and I did not explode. Amazing. But I did think of one sad thing about the summer. My little brother, Andrew, would not be able to share it with me. I guess I had better explain about my two houses, and why I am usually a two-two.

Only One House

I am usually a two-two because I usually have two houses, two mommies, two daddies, two best friends, two stuffed cats, and two bicycles. You name it, I probably have two of them. I even wear two different pairs of glasses. The blue ones are for reading. The pink ones are for the rest of the time.

This is how I got to be a two-two: A long time ago, I lived in the big house all the time. Back then it was just me, Mommy, Daddy, my little brother, Andrew, and Daddy's cranky cat, Boo-Boo. Then Mommy and Daddy got a divorce, which meant they were not married to each other anymore. So Mommy moved into a little house not far away. (It is next door to Nancy's house.) Andrew and I went with Mommy. Daddy stayed in the big house because it is the house he grew up in.

Then Mommy got married again, to a very nice man named Seth Engle. That makes Seth my stepfather. He came to live with us in the little house. He brought his cat, Midgie, and his dog, Rocky.

Then Daddy got married again too, to Kristy's mommy, Elizabeth Thomas. Elizabeth's kids are Sam and Charlie, who are in high school; Kristy, who is thirteen (I just adore Kristy); and David Michael, who is seven, like me. But he does not go to my school.

Then Daddy and Elizabeth adopted my little sister, Emily Michelle, from a country called Vietnam. Emily is two and a half.

There were so many people at the big house that Nannie, Elizabeth's mother, came to help take care of everyone. Nannie also helps out with the pets. Kristy has a new puppy named Scout. She will keep her for a year. Then Scout will go to guide dog school. Plus, David Michael has a puppy named Shannon, and of course there is Boo-Boo, and our fish, and Andrew's pet hermit crab, and my pet rat, Emily Junior. The big house is always pretty noisy and exciting.

At first, Andrew and I stayed at the little house most of the time. We lived at the big house only every other weekend. But Andrew and I wanted to see our big-house family more often. So Mommy and Daddy talked, and their lawyers talked. Everyone agreed that Andrew and I could live at the little house one month, and at the big house the next month. So we did that, and everyone was much happier. *Then* Seth was offered a job for six months in Chicago, which is a big city far away. (The big and little houses are in Stoneybrook, Connecticut.)

Well. I could not decide whether to go with Mommy and Seth and Andrew to

Chicago for six months, or to stay at the big house for six months. (Mommy decided that Andrew was too little to be away from her for six whole months. After all, he is only four going on five. But I am much older than he is. So I had to decide for myself.)

I tried Chicago. But I was not happy there. I did not want to go to a new school. I wanted my same old room and my same old friends and my same old Ms. Colman and my same old street and my same old neighborhood. So I came back to Stoney-brook. And I am very glad I did. I do miss Mommy and Andrew and Seth *a lot*. But we write and call and send e-mail all the time. And I will visit them for a whole month soon. So I am doing fine.

Anyway. Now that I am at the big house for awhile, my life is a lot simpler. I do not have to think about changing houses. And the big house is always fun and full of people. Right now it was full of my family and my two best friends as we ate lunch.

There are so many of us at the big house that we eat at a long, long table with two long, long benches. Today I was sitting between Hannie and Nancy. Nannie had made a gigundo pile of tuna-salad sandwiches. Plus we had carrot sticks and apple slices and glasses of milk and afterward two chocolate chip cookies each.

"What is everyone going to do this afternoon?" asked Daddy. (He works at home. Elizabeth works in an office, which is why she was not eating lunch with us.)

"I am going to look for a job," said Charlie. "I need gas money this summer."

"I am going to look for a job too," said Sam. "There are a bunch of CDs I want to buy. And the paper route does not pay enough."

"Okay," said Daddy.

"I have a baby-sitting job," said Kristy. (She runs a baby-sitting business with her friends. She is an excellent baby-sitter.)

"I am going to play with Scott and Timmy Hsu," said David Michael. (They live down the street from us.)

I looked at Hannie and Nancy. "We are going to hang out and enjoy the summer," I said.

"Sounds like a good plan," said Daddy.

So the other two Musketeers and I put a few more cookies in our pockets, and headed outside to start enjoying the summer.

Daddy's Vacation Plan

Sometimes enjoying summer can be hard work. Running around in the sun and riding bikes and climbing trees can wear you out. After doing those things in the big-house neighborhood for a few days, Hannie and I went to Nancy's house. (It was weird seeing my little house next door without going in it. But another family was renting it while my little-house family was in Chicago.)

At Nancy's house we worked very hard on our mud-pie bakery all afternoon. We were not making little-kid-type mud pies.

13

They were much better than that. We decorated our pies with flowers and pebbles and twigs and moss, and baked them in the sun, and served them on beautiful shiny leaf-platters. And we used only the finest dirt, and fresh water right from the hose.

I was exhausted by the time I went home.

That night at dinner I could barely keep my eyes open long enough to eat. (I had already taken a bath and was wearing my pajamas.) My big-house family was gathered around our table, eating lamb chops and corn on the cob and fresh green beans. I was eating with one hand and propping my head up with my other hand.

Then Daddy tapped his water glass with his fork. "Ahem," he said. "I have a question to ask. Elizabeth and I thought it would be fun to go on a family vacation together, starting not this Friday but the Friday after that. We would like to go to Shadow Lake. Does that sound like a good idea?"

"Yes!" I shouted. Suddenly I felt wide-awake. Daddy has a vacation house at a ski resort called Shadow Lake. It is in western Massachusetts, about two hours away from Stoneybrook. When it is too hot to snow-ski, you can go there for fishing and water-skiing and hiking and all sorts of fun things. I love going to Shadow Lake.

"Sounds good to me," said Kristy.

"I want to go," said David Michael.

"Boys?" asked Daddy. He looked at Sam and Charlie.

"Well," said Charlie.

"Um," said Sam. "Actually, I just got a job. I am washing dishes at the Five Happiness restaurant. I am going to start tomorrow afternoon."

"I got a job too," said Charlie. "I am going to be making deliveries for an auto-parts store. I do not think I should miss a week of work to go to Shadow Lake. Even though I love Shadow Lake."

"Me too," said Sam. "I wish I could postpone taking this job. But I am afraid they

will give it to someone else. Can I stay home with Charlie while you go to Shadow Lake?"

"Stay home?" asked Elizabeth. "By yourselves?"

"I am seventeen," said Charlie. "Sam is fifteen. We are old enough to be responsible here by ourselves for a week. Besides, someone has to stay home to take care of Scout. Right?"

"I was going to take Scout with me," said Kristy.

"If Scout goes, then Shannon should go too," said David Michael.

"And Emily Jr.," I said.

"I think all the pets should stay here," said Daddy.

"Then can we stay here to care for the pets?" asked Sam.

Elizabeth looked at Daddy. Daddy looked at Elizabeth.

"We will need time to think about this," said Elizabeth. "We will talk it over and discuss it later, okay? Now, how about every-one else?"

"Actually, dear," said Nannie, "I have a very big order coming up. . . ."

Nannie has her own chocolate-making business.

"If you need to stay home, that is okay," said Elizabeth.

"There!" said Charlie. "Nannie will be home too. Now can Sam and I stay here?"

"We will think about it," said Daddy.

"Can I ask Mary Anne to come with us?" asked Kristy. (Mary Anne is Kristy's best friend. She is gigundoly nice. She is a little bit shy. I am not shy.)

"Can I ask Hannie and Nancy to come too?" I said. I was so excited that I was bouncing up and down. Hannie and Nancy had come to Shadow Lake once before. I knew they would want to come again.

"Can I ask Scott and Timmy Hsu to come?" asked David Michael.

"Me! Me!" said Emily Michelle. She tried

to stand up in her high chair. Her sippy cup tipped over but did not spill.

Elizabeth laughed. "Yes, honey, you will definitely go."

Daddy took a breath. "I did not think our vacation plans would get so complicated," he said. "Although I should have suspected it. But Elizabeth and I will talk it all out, and we will tell you our decisions tomorrow."

I could barely sit still. Hannie and Nancy just *had* to come to Shadow Lake. They just *had* to!

All Girls!

The next day Daddy and Elizabeth said they had decided that I could ask Hannie and Nancy to come to Shadow Lake with us. Kristy could ask Mary Anne, and David Michael could ask Scott and Timmy Hsu. And Charlie and Sam could stay home with Nannie and take care of all the pets.

Everyone was very happy about all these things.

"I can come!" Hannie yelled from across the street. She looked both ways very carefully. No cars were coming. So she scooted across to where I waited on the other side.

"I can come!" Hannie yelled again.

We grabbed hands and jumped up and down. "Yea!" I cried. I could feel my ponytail flapping against my back.

"Yea!" Hannie said. We jumped up and down until we felt we could stand the excitement.

"Come on," I said. "I need some lemonade. Then we can talk about Shadow Lake."

Once we had our lemonade, we went into the backyard and sat down in the glider swing on the patio. We swung our legs back and forth.

"Nancy called this morning," I said. "She can come too. So the Three Musketeers will be together at Shadow Lake."

"Hooray!" Hannie cried. "This is going to be so much fun. I loved being at Shadow Lake last time."

"Me too," I said.

"Did you know that we will be there until Father's Day?" asked Hannie.

I nodded. "Father's Day is on a Sunday. There is a fishing contest at Shadow Lake that day. Then we will come home on Monday morning."

"It is too bad I will not be home with my daddy on Father's Day," said Hannie.

"That is what Nancy said too," I told her. "But maybe we can call your daddies on Sunday, and wish them a happy Father's Day."

"Good idea," said Hannie.

Later on Nancy called again. Hannie picked up the phone in the playroom. I picked up the phone in the hall outside my bedroom. We both talked to Nancy at the same time. Together, we planned what clothes and books and games we would take to Shadow Lake. We decided we would each bring *all* of our bathing suits. We decided we would each take one book, and then switch them around. It took us a long time to agree on which three books we wanted.

Then Hannie had to go home for lunch.

After lunch I went to my room and pulled my big suitcase out from under my bed. I wanted to start getting ready, even though our trip was still two weeks away.

Kristy came into my room and put a pile of clean laundry on my bed. "Remember to take lots of shorts and shirts," she said. "And maybe one or two nice dresses."

"Okay," I replied. "Did you know Hannie and Nancy are coming?"

"Great!" said Kristy. "Mary Anne is coming also. We will have fun together."

"With Scott and Timmy too," I said. "They have never been to Shadow Lake before. They will have a great time."

"Actually," said Kristy, "they are not coming. And neither is David Michael. When David Michael asked them, it turned out their family had already planned to go to Adventure Land that week. So instead of coming with us, David Michael is going with *them*. He will not come to Shadow Lake."

"Gee," I said. "I love Adventure Land. But I am happy to be going to Shadow Lake with you and Mary Anne and Hannie and Nancy." Then I had a thought. "Guess what, Kristy? David Michael is not coming. Sam and Charlie are not coming. Andrew is in Chicago. There will be *no boys* at Shadow Lake!"

Kristy thought for a moment. "Except Watson." (Watson is my daddy.) "But you are right," Kristy continued. "There will not be any other boys with us."

We looked at each other. We grinned. Then we slapped high fives.

"No boys! Hooray!" we cried.

On the Road

Not the next Friday but the Friday after *that*, I hopped out of bed early. Today was the day! I scrambled into my clothes fast and brushed my hair and pulled it into a ponytail. Then I ran downstairs and grabbed an apple-cinnamon muffin for breakfast.

After breakfast we began to load Daddy's van and Elizabeth's station wagon. (The last time we went to Shadow Lake, there had been so many people, we could barely fit into *three* cars.)

The Three Musketeers were going in Daddy's van. Sam helped me carry my suitcase to the back of the van. Kristy, Mary Anne, and Emily Michelle were going in Elizabeth's car. There was already a pile of suitcases by the back of the station wagon.

"Hi!" called Hannie. She and Mrs. Papadakis were crossing the street. Mrs. Papadakis carried Hannie's suitcase. "I have already said good-bye to my daddy and to Linny and Sari," Hannie told me. (Linny is Hannie's brother. He is nine. Sari is her sister. She is a little bit younger than Emily Michelle.)

Mrs. Papadakis put down Hannie's suitcase and talked to Daddy about the trip.

Two minutes later Nancy's parents dropped her off with her suitcase. She kissed them good-bye. She kissed her baby brother, Danny, good-bye. Then Hannie kissed her mother good-bye. Then I kissed Sam, Charlie, and Nannie good-bye. (I did not kiss David Michael, but we shook hands.) After all that kissing, my lips felt tingly.

Then the cars were loaded, and we were off!

First we drove through Stoneybrook. Then we drove through the rest of Connecticut. We crossed the state line into Massachusetts. (There is no real line that you can see. Just a sign that says, "Welcome to Massachusetts.") Then we drove across Massachusetts till we reached Shadow Lake.

Two hours is a long time, but it passed pretty quickly. First we sang all the songs we knew. Daddy listened to music from the radio. He turned it up loud.

Then we played guessing games and I Spy and Aunt Agnes Went to Africa. Then we stopped at a rest stop and used the rest rooms and bought some peanut-butter crackers. After we had eaten our crackers and run around for five minutes, Daddy called us back to the van.

We sang more songs. We talked about every single person in Ms. Colman's class. Then Daddy said, "If you were stuck on a deserted island with only three other people from Ms. Colman's class, who would you want them to be?" I chose Hannie, Nancy, and Sara Ford. Hannie chose me and Nancy and Audrey Green. Nancy chose me and Hannie and Omar Harris.

Then Hannie and I teased Nancy for the rest of the trip about Omar being her boyfriend.

Finally we turned off the main road onto a smaller road. We were surrounded by beautiful woods with pine trees and maples and sycamores and oaks.

"There it is!" I said, pointing out the window. "I see the lodge!"

Shadow Lake is very busy in the wintertime, because people go there to ski. So there is a big lodge with a restaurant and a gift shop and a game room and a library and just about anything you could want.

Our house is down the road a little, on the other side of the lodge.

"Hello, lodge!" said Hannie.

"Good-bye, lodge!" said Nancy as we drove past it.

That cracked me up.

Then Daddy turned into our driveway, and I saw our house.

The Three Musketeers cheered.

"Please wait until I stop the car before you leap out," said Daddy.

As soon as he stopped, we flung open our doors and jumped out. The three of us ran up the stairs and raced up and down the shaded porch.

"We are here! We are here!" I sang. Then I threw my arms wide. "Let our vacation begin!"

The Three Musketeer
Hotel

Daddy calls his Shadow Lake house a cabin, but it is actually too big to be a cabin. It is a funny house. Inside is a huge living room. At one end is a long table with long benches, just like at home. The kitchen is at one end of the living room. So it is really the living-dining-kitchen room. There are two tiny bedrooms, barely big enough for beds and dressers. There are three little bathrooms. And there are also two huge bedrooms. Get this: Each of the two huge bedrooms has *six* bunk beds in it. So the house can hold a gigundoly lot of people.

When we are not at Shadow Lake, a man named Mitch Conway takes care of our house. When we ran through the front door we found a small vase of wildflowers on the table, and a note from Mitch saying, "Welcome!" Our house was neat and clean, as usual, and the windows had been opened to let in fresh air.

Hannie and Nancy had been here before, so they knew where everything was. The three of us ran to the girls' bedroom right away. (Girls usually sleep in one of the huge bedrooms, and boys sleep in the other.)

The bunk beds were lined up along the walls. There were three white dressers, and three little tables with lamps on them. A beautiful quilt was folded neatly at the bottom of each bed.

"The first thing we should do is make our beds," I said briskly. "I will get sheets from the linen closet."

But before we did that, Elizabeth's car pulled up and she honked the horn. We all ran outside to welcome the rest of our all-girl party.

"Hello! Hello!" I called as Elizabeth, Emily Michelle, Kristy, and Mary Anne got out of the station wagon.

"Hello!" said Elizabeth. She set Emily down, and my little sister started climbing the steps up to the porch.

We helped them unload everything. Inside, Kristy and Mary Anne headed for the girls' room, but then stopped in the middle of the living room.

"I forgot," said Kristy. "There are no boys here. We can have the other bedroom. All right!"

"That's true," said Elizabeth. "You guys can really spread out."

Kristy and Mary Anne headed for the room where the boys usually sleep. Which meant . . .

"Come on!" I said to Hannie and Nancy. We ran back to our bedroom. "This room is *all ours!*" I twirled around on the middle of a braided rug. "I have never been here before when I did not have to share this room with nineteen million other people. But it is just us three here. This is our private room!"

Hannie and Nancy smiled.

"It is like having a hotel room all to ourselves," said Nancy. "The Three Musketeer Hotel."

"We can stay up late and whisper and play with our flashlights," said Hannie. "Kristy will not be here to remind us to go to sleep."

The three of us looked at each other. I felt so excited, I could not stand it. Our vacation was getting better and better all the time!

"There are twelve different beds," said Nancy. "I cannot choose which one I want. We could all sleep in top bunks. Or all sleep in bottom bunks."

"I know!" I said. I had just gotten a great idea. "We can each have a new bed every night. We will switch around."

"Yes!" said Hannie.

"Top bunks first!" said Nancy.

So we each picked out a top bunk and made it up with fresh sheets. We were all set.

"Girls?" called Elizabeth. "I am going to the grocery store in town. Would you like to come with me, to help me shop?"

"Yes!" we said, and scrambled off our bunks. Outside we piled into Elizabeth's car. The air smelled like pine trees. The sun was shining. I felt very, very happy.

Keegan (A Boy)

The Shadow Lake grocery store is not a gigundo supermarket, like the one back in Stoneybrook. It is more like a small general store, with many fascinating things, such as fishing poles and lures, bait, water toys, tin buckets for picking blueberries, and home-made pies and jams.

While Elizabeth filled her basket with milk, bread, cereal, cheese, and other food we would need, Hannie and Nancy and I looked at all the things on the shelves.

"This says gooseberry jam," Nancy said. "What's a gooseberry?"

Hannie and I did not know. I pictured a berry shaped like a goose, or maybe just a berry that geese like to eat. I was thinking about this when I heard someone call my name.

"Karen! Karen Brewer!"

I turned around and saw a boy standing in the next aisle.

"Keegan!" I said happily. I had met Keegan at Shadow Lake one time when my family had come to snow-ski. I had not liked skiing very much, and neither had Keegan. We had hung out at the lodge together.

"Hannie, Nancy!" I said. "This is my friend Keegan. Keegan, meet Hannie and Nancy, my two best friends."

"Hi," said Hannie. She gave a tiny smile.

"Hi," said Nancy. She did not smile at all.

I wondered what was going on.

"Are you going to be here long?" Keegan asked.

"Uh-huh. Until the Monday after Father's Day," I said. "We are going to fish in the fishing contest. What about you?"

"I will be here for another week," said Keegan. "We have been here a week already."

"Great," I said. "Then we will have lots of time to do stuff together. Remember when we played video games at the lodge?"

"Yeah," said Keegan. "And we had that great snowball fight."

"Karen, girls, I am ready to leave," said Elizabeth.

"We have to go now. But we can play together soon," I told Keegan.

"Okay. See you later!" he said.

Nancy and Hannie did not say a thing.

Our house at Shadow Lake has its own dock that reaches out over the water. I am not allowed to play on the dock unless Kristy or a grown-up is with me. That afternoon, Hannie and Nancy and I were all sitting on the dock. We were dangling our bare feet over the water. Kristy and Mary Anne sat at the other end of the dock with Emily Michelle. Emily Michelle had a pocketful of pebbles. She was dropping them into the lake one by one. Daddy and Elizabeth were making barbecue for dinner. Yum!

"Daddy says he has three fishing poles he can lend us," I said. "We can use them in the fishing contest."

"We should practice fishing," Hannie said. "I am not very good at it."

"Let's practice every single day," said Nancy. "For at least an hour."

"Good idea," I said. "We can start tomorrow. I bet we will be good fishers by the end of the week. I would like to win a prize in the fishing contest. Maybe for the biggest fish."

"Or the most beautiful fish," said Nancy.

"Maybe tomorrow we can go swimming," said Hannie. "After we practice fishing."

"We can go swimming, or play in our secret house, or take a walk through the woods, or go to the lodge," I said. "I know! We should write down all our choices, and then schedule them. I will run to the house and get a piece of paper —"

"No, Karen," said Hannie. She was laughing. "No schedules. We will just decide to do things when we feel like it."

"What if we forget to do something fun?" I asked.

"We will not forget," said Nancy. "Trust me."

"Okaaaay." I sat down again. So they won. "We have to remember to call Keegan tomorrow," I said. "He is very nice. He could come over and practice fishing with us."

"Um," said Hannie. She looked at Nancy. Nancy looked at Hannie.

"What," I said.

"Well, Karen," said Nancy. "Keegan is a *boy*. This is a no-boys week, remember?"

Then I realized why Hannie and Nancy had not been very friendly to Keegan in the grocery store.

"After all," said Hannie. "I thought this would be a special Three Musketeers week. Not a Three Musketeers and a boy week."

For just a second, I felt a tiny bit angry at Hannie and Nancy. Keegan was a friend of mine. I did not want to be mean to him. I thought Hannie and Nancy were being selfish. But I remembered something Nannie had told me once: If you are angry, count to twenty before you speak. So I did. You know what? It worked. I was not so angry anymore.

"I understand," I said. "But I do not want to hurt Keegan's feelings. Would it be okay if this is a mostly all-girls week with just a little bit of boy?"

Hannie and Nancy thought about it.

Finally they nodded. "Okay," said Hannie. "Just a little bit of boy. I do not want you to hurt Keegan's feelings."

"But he cannot come to our secret house," replied Nancy. "That is still for girls only."

I smiled. "Thank you," I said to my best friends. "No boys in the secret house."

The Secret House

We started practicing our fishing the very next morning after breakfast. Daddy came with us to the dock. Kristy and Mary Anne set off on a walk. Elizabeth took Emily Michelle to play on the tiny strip of sandy beach nearby.

Daddy showed us how to put little pieces of raw shrimp on our hooks without poking our fingers. Then we dropped our lines in the water and waited. When our bobbers bobbed in the water, we knew fish were nibbling our bait. We yanked up our lines, but again and again nothing was there.

"Those pesky fish are eating our bait without getting caught," I said.

"They are very smart fish," Nancy grumbled.

After an hour of not catching anything, we decided practice was over. We had given about a million fish a nice breakfast.

"Just you wait," I said, shaking my fist at the water. "I will catch one of you yet."

After practice the Three Musketeers headed into the woods to our little secret house.

"Go only to your house, no farther," said Daddy. "I want to be able to see you right away."

"Okay, Daddy," I said.

We had found the secret house the last time we were here. It is really just an abandoned shed, but it makes a great playhouse. On our last vacation here, we had cleaned it up and put curtains in the windows.

"Ew. It is all dusty again," said Hannie.

"We can pretend that we just woke up after sleeping for a hundred years," I said. "Like Sleeping Beauty. There is a hundred years' worth of dust all over everything. So we have to clean it up."

"My name is Princess Aurora," said Nancy. She brushed her long hair back over her shoulder. "Oh, I am all stiff and sore after sleeping for so long."

It was a great game. I was Princess Marigold. Hannie was Princess Annamaria. We were Sleeping Beauties until lunchtime.

After a delicious lunch of hot dogs, Kristy asked us if we wanted to walk to the lodge.

"Mary Anne and I are going to the game room," she said.

"Count us in!" I said.

The lodge is like a big hotel, but with no bedrooms. First we looked in the gift store. We saw magazines and candy and gum and sunscreen lotion and even paperback books. We bought postcards to send to people in Stoneybrook.

"I will send this one to my daddy," said

Hannie. "I am a little sad that I will not see him on Father's Day."

"Me too," said Nancy. "I will send my daddy this one."

I felt bad that my friends were sad about their daddies. "Hey!" I said. "I think we should go to the game room and find Kristy and Mary Anne." I wanted Hannie and Nancy to think of something besides Father's Day.

In the game room, some older kids were playing pool. I do not know how to play pool. I think I am too short. Some kids were playing video games. Kristy and Mary Anne had started a game of Monopoly with some other kids. I knew Kristy would cream them.

For awhile Nancy and Hannie and I played Parcheesi. Then we played video games. Then the Ping-Pong table was free, so we ran to it. We each picked up a paddle.

"Uh-oh," I said. "There are only three of us. That is two against one. That is not fair."

"We could take turns," said Nancy. "One

of us could wait, and then play the winner."

"That could take forever," said Hannie.

Then I spotted Keegan standing by a video game.

"I have an idea," I said. "We could ask Keegan to play with us. Then we will be two against two. Is that okay?"

Hannie and Nancy decided it was okay. Keegan was happy to play with us. We played until dinnertime.

"You are right," said Hannie as we walked home with Kristy and Mary Anne. "Keegan is a nice boy."

"I am glad you think so," I said.

The Monster of
Shadow Lake

That night Hannie and Nancy and I decided to sleep in three bottom bunks close to our window. Unmaking beds and making new beds was kind of a pain, but it was fun switching where we slept each night. And it was sooo much fun having the room to ourselves. We could stay up very late, talking, as long as we were pretty quiet.

After we had taken our turns in the shower, we put on our pajamas and sat on our beds. We were all untangling our hair.

"At home my mommy untangles my hair," said Hannie. "I think I am a little bit homesick. Not that I am not having a good time," she said quickly. "I am having a great time. And I am happy to be with you and Nancy. But I also like being at home with Mommy and Daddy. And even Linny and Sari."

"I know what you mean," I said. "It is weird. Sometimes when I am at the big house, I miss the little house. And when I am at the little house, I miss the big house. I cannot help it."

"We should not think about anything sad," said Nancy. "We are together now, all for one and one for all. We can have a good time."

"You are right," I said. I was so glad they were here with me. It is great to be able to share all your feelings — even sad ones — with your best friends.

"Hey, I smell . . . " I sniffed the air.

"Popcorn!" we all said at once. We jumped up and ran out into the living room.

Daddy was popping corn over our fireplace, which had a real fire in it. (Even during the summer, sometimes it can be a little chilly at night at Shadow Lake. That is because it is in the mountains.)

"You are just in time," said Kristy. "Watson is going to tell us stories about when he was little and he came here to Shadow Lake."

"Goody!" I said. I pulled some cushions off the couch, and Hannie and Nancy and I curled up on them. We made sure we were within reach of the popcorn bowl.

Elizabeth came out of one of the tiny bedrooms. "Emily is finally asleep, thank goodness. I think all this fresh air is giving her more energy than usual." Elizabeth collapsed into an armchair and smiled at Daddy.

Daddy told us many funny stories about when he was a little boy. He told us about learning to fish with his uncle. He told us about some of the people he had met here during the summers. And he told us

about . . . the Shadow Lake Monster!

I had found out about the Lake Monster the first time I was here. Some people say (and I think I believe them) that there is a sea monster in Shadow Lake. Like the Loch Ness Monster. Maybe it is one last dinosaur that never died out. I do not know.

This time Daddy talked about different people who claimed they had seen it. I had not seen it myself when I was here. But now I was getting an idea.

I waited until the Three Musketeers were back in our own room. We climbed into bed. Elizabeth came in to make sure we were tucked in, and she kissed me good night and turned off the light. As soon as she had closed the door behind her, I rolled over in bed.

"Hey!" I whispered. "Are you guys awake?"

"Of course we are," whispered Hannie. "Elizabeth just turned off the light a second ago."

"I had an idea," I said softly.

"Uh-oh." Nancy groaned. "Sometimes your ideas mean trouble."

Hannie giggled. I knew Nancy was just teasing me.

"Listen," I said. "Every morning we will be out on the dock to practice fishing, right? So from now on, I will take a camera with me. If there is a Lake Monster, sooner or later it will have to come up for air. I will be right there with my camera. And I can be the first person to get a picture of the monster! We can all be famous!"

"That is a pretty good plan," said Nancy reluctantly.

"I think we should do it," said Hannie.

"Okay," I said. "Tomorrow I will bring my camera."

Poor Fishing

Guess what. I brought my camera with us on Sunday, Monday, and Tuesday. I did not once see the Lake Monster. Not only that, but I did not catch any fish. And neither did Hannie or Nancy. We were getting discouraged.

"Maybe we are using the wrong kind of bait," Hannie said on Tuesday morning.

"Let's try something else," I said.

We tried little pieces of bologna. The fish loved them. I felt my line jerk, and my bobber went under the water. But when I pulled up my pole, the fish was gone — and so was the bologna.

Then we started trying everything we could think of: acorns, cheese, little pieces of apple, stale popcorn. The fish loved it all. They just did not wait around to see who was feeding them the delicious meal.

"We are definitely going to lose the fishing contest," I said. I did not really mind. We were only entering the contest for fun. But it would be really neat to be able to catch some fish.

"Maybe you should try live worms, or night crawlers," said Daddy.

Hannie and Nancy and I wrinkled our noses.

"I do not think so," I said politely. "Maybe we will try bread with peanut butter on it."

"Okay," said Daddy.

Besides the bait problem, we were also having trouble keeping our lines untangled. Each day we started off far apart, so we would not get in one another's way. But that made it hard to talk. Slowly, we edged closer and closer to one another. Then all of a sudden, our lines were tangled up. Or we would hit one another with our poles. Once Nancy even got her hook caught on the back of my shirt!

"Do not move!" she cried to me. I froze like a statue. "Mr. Brewer!" called Nancy. "Mr. Brewer, help!"

Daddy carefully unhooked me. I did not even have a scratch. "Well, Nancy, this is the biggest fish anyone has caught yet," said Daddy.

Nancy giggled.

At least we were not the only ones not catching fish. Daddy and Mary Anne and Kristy could not catch anything either. In fact, the only person who did catch anything was . . . Emily Michelle!

Elizabeth had bought Emily a small toy fishing pole with a safe plastic hook. Emily loved dangling it in the water.

"I fishin'!" she said happily. "I fishin' too!"

At first we just smiled at her. Then her eyes grew round, and her pole jerked a little bit.

"Mommy! Mommy!" she said. "Fish!"

We all turned to look at her. I thought she had gotten her hook caught on a weed or something. But Elizabeth pulled up Emily Michelle's line to untangle it. On the hook was a small sunfish!

It was too small to eat. After we had admired it and praised Emily, Elizabeth slipped the fish back into the water and let it swim away.

"No!" yelled Emily. "My fishie! My fishie!"

Hannie and Nancy and I helped Elizabeth explain that the fish had to go home to its mommy so it could grow bigger.

"You will catch another one," I promised.

Emily Michelle frowned and looked very determined. She dropped her line back in the water. Hannie and Nancy and I decided to go to the lodge for awhile.

* * *

"Hey, look at this," said Kristy at dinnertime. She held up a fishing lure against her ear. "It is an earring!"

We all laughed. A fishing lure is something you can attach to your hook to get a fish's attention. Sometimes you use it with no bait. Sometimes you put bait on it. Lures can look like plastic worms or bugs, or they can be shiny metal, or little corks with feathers on them. Real feathers.

The one Kristy held up was pretty. It was red and black and white, with a small red-and-white feather.

"You know what?" said Mary Anne. "That is not a bad earring. Really. Hold up another one."

Kristy held up one lure against each ear and smiled.

Mary Anne looked thoughtful. "Hmm," she said.

Lures

"We have to get serious about the Lake Monster, guys," I said on Wednesday afternoon. After not catching anything that morning, we had walked to the lodge. We bought a package of M&M's and shared them. Then we headed home.

On our way we passed Kristy and Mary Anne and their new business. Yup. You guessed it. They had started to make earrings out of lures. Mary Anne was wearing a pair, as an advertisement. She and Kristy had set up a small card table outside the lodge entrance. A poster said A-LURE-ING EARRINGS BY MAK. MAK meant Mary Anne and Kristy.

"How is business?" I asked.

"It is great!" Kristy said. "Mary Anne is making the earrings. I am handling the advertising and the supplies. Everyone wants a pair of A-lure-ing Earrings. We have sold four pairs so far."

Mary Anne grinned at us. She had borrowed wire cutters and a pair of pliers from Daddy. First she snipped off the pointy hook from a lure. Then she slipped another wire through the loop and bent it. Then she had an earring.

"I just hope our supplies hold out," said Kristy. "We might have to go into the next town and buy all *their* fishing lures."

We looked at their sample earrings. They were very pretty and definitely unusual. We wished Mary Anne and Kristy good luck, and went home.

* * *

"I mean it. We have to get serious about the Lake Monster," I said again.

"How?" asked Nancy.

"Maybe one hour of watching for it is not enough," said Hannie.

"Do you want to spend all day looking for it?" asked Nancy.

"Yes!" I said. "If we cannot catch any fish, at least we can catch a terrific photo of the Lake Monster."

With Daddy's help, we made a shelter for ourselves by the side of the lake. We piled big leafy branches against a tree. It made a small cave just big enough for the three of us to sit inside.

The next day, we skipped fishing practice. (To tell you the truth, I was glad to miss a day.) Hannie and Nancy and I crawled into our little shelter. We were each wearing green or brown clothes, so the Lake Monster could not see us if he glanced our way.

"Okay," I whispered. "Operation Lake

Monster is officially underway." I checked my clipboard. "Hannie, do you have your sketchpad?"

"Check," Hannie whispered.

"Nancy, do you have our lunches?" I asked.

"Check," said Nancy.

"And I have our camera. So we are all set," I said.

If you have never been on a stakeout before, you might not know that it is fun for the first twenty minutes, and then very, very boring.

By ten o'clock in the morning our legs were stiff. Hannie was yawning. Nancy was drawing pictures of all of us with different hairstyles.

"Maybe some food would help me wake up," said Hannie. "Is it lunchtime yet?"

I checked my watch. "It is five minutes after ten."

We ate our lunches anyway.

I tried to keep my eyes on the water at all times. It was a cloudy day, but I could see

every ripple. Several times I saw a small splash, but twice it was fish, and once it was a duck. I was afraid if I looked away for a second, that would be when the Lake Monster would poke its head out of the water.

"Maybe we should make sure our camera is working," I said. We took a couple of goofy pictures of one another. After another half hour, I decided anything as big as the Lake Monster would definitely get my attention even if I looked away for a second. So we played hangman for awhile on our sketchpad.

Hannie won, with the word *holiday*.

We all jumped when we heard a big crack of thunder overhead.

I looked at Hannie. Hannie looked at Nancy. Nancy looked at me.

"Great, just great," I said.

Then it began to pour.

Footsteps in the Rain

I had started to think that a stakeout for the Lake Monster was not such a good idea. After all, we were on vacation. It is not much fun just to sit all day, watching, when we could be playing.

The stakeout was especially not fun once it started to rain.

Our shelter was not rainproof. Water dripped through the leaves and branches and landed on our heads. But I did not want to quit yet. I am not a quitter. Hannie and Nancy are not quitters either. So we sat there and got wet. I kept my eyes on the lake.

"Sometimes rain makes me feel sad," said Hannie.

"Me too," I said. "When it rains, I like being all cozy at home."

"With hot chocolate and maybe popcorn," said Nancy.

"And my daddy," said Hannie.

"I am just so sad that I will not be with my daddy on Father's Day," said Nancy.

"Me too," said Hannie.

I did not say anything, because I *would* be with my daddy on Father's Day. I felt bad that my friends would not. But it was because of the big fishing contest on Sunday, which we absolutely could not miss. Otherwise we could just go home early. That fishing contest was ruining everything. But I could not ask Daddy to leave before Sunday. He was looking forward to the contest. It is the kind of thing that daddies like. Too bad Mr. Papadakis and Mr. Dawes could not be in the fishing contest, I thought. They would probably like it.

Then I sat up straight. My eyes grew big. I was hatching one of my gigundoly brilliant ideas.

"What?" asked Hannie. "What is it? Do you see something?" She peered out through the rain at the lake.

"Um, no, I do not see anything," I said quickly. "I thought I did, but I was wrong."

Nancy looked at me suspiciously. I tried to act casual.

The rain dripped steadily down. I was very excited about my idea, and wanted to run back to the house to talk to Daddy about it. Also, I was fed up with the Lake Monster. If the monster was not even going to peek its head out on a gloomy, rainy day, then I was going to give up.

Just then Nancy grabbed my arm. "Shhh!" she whispered, although I had not said anything.

"What —" I started to say, then clamped

my hand over my mouth. I heard it! I heard footsteps! Footsteps were crunching closer and closer to us!

"Could the Lake Monster be out of the lake?" whispered Hannie, her eyes round.

I had not thought of that. I felt my heart start to beat faster, as if I had been running. I pictured the huge, slimy Lake Monster, dripping with water, plodding through the woods. He would smell us! He would think, Gee, three nice little girls. What a good lunch they would be.

Daddy would not see us being eaten. Our little shelter would hide us from his view.

Hannie and Nancy and I held hands.

Suddenly a blond head poked around the edge of our shelter. I almost screamed.

"What are you guys doing?" asked Keegan.

Well. Talk about relief.

Keegan was completely soaked, like we were. He held a tin bucket in one hand and a small trowel in the other. His hands were muddy.

"Um, we are just playing," I said. "What are *you* doing?"

"I am digging up worms and night crawlers," said Keegan. "They make the best bait for fishing. And in the rain is the best time to find them." He looked at us huddled in our shelter, sopping wet. "Do you all want to help me?"

It did not take us long to say yes.

Worms, Worms, Everywhere

Here are some things worms are:

Wiggly
Orangey-pink
Really slimy
Mild-mannered
Stretchy

Keegan had some spare coffee cans for us to put our captured worms in. He was right:

In the rain is the best time to find worms. I guess they get thirsty, just like everything else. We did not have to look very hard to find about a million plump pink worms poking their heads out of the dirt.

"I found one, I found one!" cried Hannie. Her long brown pigtails were streaming wetly down her back.

"Okay," said Keegan.

We gathered around Hannie's worm.

"First, clear away the leaves and stuff, so you can see it," instructed Keegan.

Hannie did.

"Now, try to scrape away the dirt around it with your hands," he said.

"Why can't she use the trowel?" I asked.

"Worms are delicate," explained Keegan. "The trowel might hurt them."

Oh.

Hannie scraped away the dirt around the worm. Now we could see almost all of it. I have to tell you, it was pretty yucky. Worms are nice creatures, and they are good for plants because they stir up the soil. But they are pretty yucky, all the same.

"Now, put a handful of dirt in your coffee can," said Keegan. "And find a short stick. Scoop the worm up over the stick, very carefully. And put it in your can."

The worm was so wiggly that it took Hannie about five tries to get it into her can. Finally she did, and we all cheered.

After that Nancy and I knew how to hunt for worms. So we wandered in circles around our house, turning over leaves and scooping up worms. It was not long before I had practically a whole coffee can full of dirt and worms.

"What are we going to do with these?" asked Hannie.

"I am going to sell them to the grocery store," said Keegan. "Then the woman at the store will sell them to people who want to use them as bait."

"I think I will keep mine," I said. "I will hide them. Then I will give Daddy the whole can on Father's Day. It will be his gift, and he can use them for fishing."

Hannie and Nancy gave theirs to Keegan.

"I do not really need all these worms," said Nancy. "I am still using bologna as fish bait."

"Oh, fish love bologna," said Keegan.

"Are you going to sign up for the fishing contest?" I asked Keegan. "We are. We will go out with my daddy on his boat."

Keegan looked uncomfortable. "Well, it is like this," he said. He shuffled his feet in the wet leaves. "My mom and dad are separated right now. They might get a divorce. So I am here with just my mom. I do not even know if I will talk to my dad on Father's Day."

Keegan looked very sad. I felt sorry for him.

"I know what it is like when your parents get divorced," I said. "It is awful. I am sorry you feel so bad right now. Hey! I know. You can come with us on our boat on Father's Day. Then you can fish with us and be in the contest."

Keegan's face brightened. "Really? Would it be all right?"

"Of course," I said. "Meet us at our dock on Sunday morning."

"Great! Thanks!" Keegan gathered up all his worms and ran off.

I felt happy that I had cheered him up. Then I had two thoughts: I had not asked Daddy for permission to ask Keegan. Oops. And I did not know how Keegan would fit in with my secret plan.

Making Cards

After breakfast on Friday, Nancy and Hannie and I sat down to make Father's Day cards. I would hand Daddy his, and I would mail one to Seth in Chicago.

We had construction paper, markers, scissors, glitter, and glue. I can make just about anything with those things.

"May we join you?" asked Kristy. "I would like to make Watson a card." (She does not ever hear from her own father.)

"Sure," I said, waving my hand. "There is plenty for everyone."

Mary Anne sat down too. She used a sheet of yellow paper. This was so nice, all of us girls together, making cards. No boys were running around, making noise. No boys were burping or singing icky songs. It was great.

Soon Emily Michelle and Elizabeth sat down too. I was glad we had brought lots of art supplies. Elizabeth helped Emily Michelle cut out things. She wrote down what Emily Michelle wanted to say on her card for Daddy.

"Do you think my card will get to my daddy tomorrow?" asked Hannie as she cut out some blue hearts. "Today is Friday. It might not get there till Monday. But I will be home on Monday afternoon. Maybe I should wait and give it to him then."

"I think you should give it to my daddy to mail today," I said firmly. "That would be the best thing."

I knew something that Hannie and Nancy did not. It was about Father's Day. The night before, while Hannie and Nancy were getting ready for bed, I had talked to Daddy and Elizabeth about my secret plan. They had thought it was a great idea. And they promised to help me.

This morning at breakfast, Elizabeth had winked at me. My plan was in motion! I was very excited about it. It was going to be sooo hard to keep it secret until tomorrow.

After our cards were made, I fed my worms breakfast. First I gathered some leaves outside. Then I put the leaves in the worms' coffee can. I had hidden the can underneath the sink in our bathroom. It was safe and dark, the way worms like things. I knew Daddy would be happy and surprised when I gave him his present.

"Karen, come on!" called Nancy. "It is time to practice fishing!"

"Coming!" I replied.

The day before, when we had abandoned our shelter, we had left some scraps from our lunches. We had set them by the water's edge, as bait for the Lake Monster. Guess what. This morning the scraps were gone.

"The Lake Monster *does* exist!" Nancy said.

"I am just glad we were not here when it snuck up and ate the scraps," said Hannie. She shivered.

"Me too," I said. It was a pretty scary thought.

We got our bait and our poles and headed for our dock to go fishing. Although I was saving worms for Daddy, I just could not use them myself. It was too yucky. Today I was using Chee•tos. They did not work very well. They melted in the water. So I borrowed some raisins from Hannie. The raisins worked great.

"I have one!" screamed Nancy. "I have a fish!"

I jumped about a foot in the air.

Hannie and I dropped our poles and ran to Nancy. Her bobber was completely underwater. She was pulling on her pole, trying to yank the fish out.

Kristy and Mary Anne dropped their poles and ran to help us. Mary Anne grabbed the net, and Kristy helped Nancy pull the line out of the water. Suddenly a pale green, flopping, jumping fish burst out of the lake.

Nancy had caught a fish!

"Oh my gosh," said Kristy as Mary Anne scooped the fish up in the net so it could not escape. "This is incredible. He is big enough to keep. Good job, Nancy."

Daddy had heard us yelling, so he ran to the dock. He took the wiggling fish off the hook and put it in a bucket. "Good for you, Nancy," he said. "We will have this fish at our big fish cookout on Sunday."

Nancy beamed.

I was so proud of her.

Can Keegan Come?

That night we went to the lodge for dinner.

The hostess smiled at Daddy and Elizabeth. "You must have left some kids at home," she said. "There are only eight of you."

We laughed. With Nannie, Sam, Charlie, David Michael, and Andrew, there would have been thirteen of us!

Once we were seated at our big table, I buttered a piece of bread. Hannie and Nancy looked very glum.

"Didn't you talk to your daddy, honey?" Elizabeth asked Nancy. Before we had left the house, Hannie and Nancy had called their daddies at home.

Nancy nodded sadly.

"Did you tell him you miss him?" I asked.

Nancy nodded. "He said he misses me too. I am having a really great time here, but I wish I could see him for Father's Day."

"Me too," said Hannie. "Although I am having a lot of fun here at Shadow Lake."

"I am sorry you are sad," I said to Hannie. "Maybe tomorrow you will feel better."

Hannie shrugged. "Tomorrow is the day before Father's Day. And I will still not be with my daddy."

"Well, maybe Karen is right," said Elizabeth. "Maybe you will feel better in the morning."

"Look!" said Kristy, pointing with her fork. "That woman is wearing a pair of A-lure-ing Earrings."

All eight of us swiveled our heads to look. Several tables away, a woman sat with her husband. A pair of blue-and-yellow lures with tiny yellow feathers dangled from her ears.

"There is another pair," said Mary Anne.

When we started looking at everyone in the restaurant, we saw at least five pairs of A-lure-ing Earrings. And Mary Anne said that a couple of people had bought more than one pair.

I was about to point out another woman who was wearing them when I realized that she was Keegan's mommy. Keegan was sitting next to her. We waved and smiled at each other.

Which reminded me.

"Oh, Daddy," I said. "I have just remembered. Keegan is here without his daddy this time. I asked him to come with us on our boat on Father's Day. Is that okay? I forgot to ask you first."

"Hmm," said Daddy. He scratched his chin. "Actually, I am not sure we will have room for Keegan."

I stared at Daddy. "Oh, no! But we have to

make room for him somehow. His parents are separated. He is so sad. I just cannot tell him that we cannot take him with us."

"Maybe we can work something out," said Elizabeth. "I bet we can find a way to fit Keegan in. Right, Watson?"

"Yes, I guess so," said Daddy with a sigh. "I have no choice but to end up with a hundred children on my boat, as usual."

We all laughed. I was relieved. Now Keegan would have a great Father's Day. And I knew that Hannie and Nancy would too. I was starting to feel like a fairy godmother.

The Surprise

On Saturday morning Hannie and Nancy both felt sad. It was a drizzly, rainy day. I almost wanted to go out to our shelter and look for the Lake Monster. Almost. But I knew that sitting in the rain would not cheer up my two best friends.

"I love being here, Karen," said Nancy. "I am glad the Three Musketeers are together. And Shadow Lake is great. But I have never been away from my daddy on Father's Day. And that is tomorrow." She sighed and looked down at her feet.

"I know," I said. "I am sorry you feel so bad. I will ask Elizabeth to make waffles for breakfast. Maybe that will help."

"Maybe so," said Hannie. (She did not look as if she believed it.) "Come on, Nancy. We cannot spoil everyone's vacation just because we feel sad."

"You are right," said Nancy. She sniffled and wiped her eyes.

Elizabeth made us blueberry waffles for breakfast. They were yummy.

After breakfast Kristy and Mary Anne went into their room to make more earrings. They could hardly keep up with the demand.

Daddy went out into the rain to practice fishing. He said fish always bite more when it is raining. We did not want to go.

"Now, I see some long faces," Elizabeth said to us, once the table had been cleared. "How about a fun art project?"

"Hooray!" I said. I love art projects.

Elizabeth gave each of us a piece of white

paper. Then she put a few drops of food coloring at the bottom. She handed us each a straw. By blowing gently through the straw at the food coloring, I made it twist and run all over the paper. It looked like a red-and-orange tree, or maybe a spiderweb.

Emily Michelle had her own piece of paper. She could not keep her fingers out of the food coloring. She ended up with rainbow fingers. "I paintin'!" she said. "I paintin'!"

But even a special art project did not cheer up Hannie and Nancy. Elizabeth looked at me, then looked at the clock. I shrugged.

Finally Nancy and Hannie and I all just flopped down on the living room couch. We listened to the rain and talked a little bit. If I had not known that Hannie and Nancy would feel much better soon, I would have gotten impatient.

Then it happened. Just before lunch, I thought I heard a car's engine. I did! Then we heard a car honking as it came up our drive.

"Who could that be?" asked Nancy.

I smiled at her. "I do not know," I said innocently.

We walked out onto the porch.

"That is my daddy's car!" cried Hannie. "It is my mommy and daddy! And Linny and Sari!"

"My mommy's car is right behind them!" said Nancy. "It is my mommy and daddy and Danny!"

They started jumping up and down.

Then another car came down our long driveway. I peered at it through the rain. It was the Pink Clinker!

I started jumping up and down too. "Nannie!" I called. "It is Nannie and Sam and David Michael and Charlie!"

For about half an hour our porch was crowded with people hugging and kissing and saying, "Surprise!"

"When Karen told us you were upset about missing Father's Day, we felt bad

too," Mr. Papadakis told Hannie. "Then Mr. Brewer invited us to the lake. So here we are."

"Oh, I am so happy," said Hannie. She hugged him, then she hugged me. "You are the best best friend ever."

Nancy hugged me too. "Thank you, Karen. This is a wonderful surprise. How did you keep it a secret?"

"It was not easy," I said, and my friends laughed.

"Who is taking care of Scout?" asked Kristy.

"My friend Dennis," said Charlie. "He is taking care of all the pets."

Here is who slept in the boys' room: Mr. Papadakis, Mr. Dawes, Sam, Charlie, David Michael, and Linny Papadakis. Here is who slept in the girls' room: the Three Musketeers, Mrs. Papadakis, Mrs. Dawes, Nannie, Kristy, and Mary Anne. (Kristy and Mary Anne had to move out of their room, but they said they did not mind.)

Emily Michelle, Sari Papadakis, and Danny Dawes slept in one of the tiny bedrooms. Daddy and Elizabeth slept in their room. So we were all set. All of us were together, cozy and snug.

Together and Apart

That afternoon the families split up to do different things. The Daweses went to the lodge. Nancy wanted to show her mommy and daddy and Danny all the fun things to do there. Mr. Dawes challenged Nancy to a game of Ping-Pong, and Mrs. Dawes wanted to look in the gift shop.

The Papadakises went for a long walk through the woods. (It had stopped raining, and the sun had come out.) Hannie promised she would not show her parents our secret house. But she did want to show them our monster-watching shelter. Linny loved the story about the Lake Monster. He and David Michael made plans to look for it later. And Linny wanted to gather leaves for his leaf collection. I told him the woods would be a good place to find leaves.

My family decided to stay home and visit. We sat around and told one another what we had been doing all week. Sam and Charlie laughed when Kristy and Mary Anne told them about the A-lure-ing Earrings. They did not laugh when Kristy told them how much money she and Mary Anne had made so far.

Sam and Charlie told us about their new summer jobs. The jobs sounded very hard and not like much fun. But Sam and Charlie were happy to have extra spending money.

Nannie said that she had been very busy with her chocolate business. "I managed to get a lot done, since I had only Sam and Charlie to look after," she said. "But the house seemed awfully big and lonely. Even Shannon and Boo-Boo seemed to wonder where everyone had gone. And I have completely forgotten how to cook for only three people! I kept making huge batches of food. But Sam and Charlie were so good and helpful. I practically felt as if I were on vacation!"

"I had a great time at Adventure Land," said David Michael. "I rode on the Scrambler at least five times."

"Oh, yeah. Your brain really needs to be more scrambled," said Sam.

David Michael looked at him. "Now I remember why I did not miss you," he said.

Elizabeth sighed and rolled her eyes.

Daddy laughed and put his arm around her. "It is great to be together again," he said.

That night *all* of us ate dinner at the lodge. We took up three large tables. Hannie and Nancy and I sat together with Mr. Dawes and Mrs. Papadakis and Sari. Sari kept bending backward in her booster seat to see Emily Michelle in *her* booster seat.

We had a delicious dinner. Sam and Charlie kept making funny jokes. We took turns counting how many ladies were wearing A-lure-ing Earrings. (There were a lot.) David Michael ordered cheesecake for dessert, but he did not like it, so he gave it to me. Yes!

Hannie and Nancy and I agreed that we had had a lot of fun during our no-boys-except-for-Keegan week. But we were glad to be with the rest of our families now. And tomorrow would be great, with the fishing contest and all of our special Father's Day plans. We would have fun all day, on our last day at Shadow Lake.

Happy Father's Day

"Psst! Wake up," said Hannie. She shook my shoulder.

"Wha?" I asked sleepily.

"It is Father's Day," Nancy whispered. "Come on, get up."

"Oh my gosh!" I said. I was instantly wide-awake. Hannie and Nancy were already dressed, even though it was very early on Sunday morning. I quickly got out of bed and got dressed quietly. (Nannie and Kristy and Mary Anne and Mrs. Papadakis and Mrs. Dawes were still asleep.)

Then the Three Musketeers sneaked out into the living room. No one else was up yet. Very quietly we set the table for breakfast. We took out our special Father's Day cards that we had made. (Daddy had not mailed Hannie's and Nancy's, since he knew their fathers were coming to the lake.) I put mine by Daddy's place. Hannie and Nancy put theirs by their daddies' places.

Then we went outside and picked some wildflowers. We put them in jelly jars on the table. They looked beautiful.

I had one last thing to do before we woke people up for breakfast. I went into the girls' bathroom and opened the cupboard door beneath the sink. I could not wait to see daddy's face when I gave him his big can of fresh worms for the fishing contest.

I reached for the can, but did not feel it. So I peered under the sink. "Oh, no!" I cried.

Instead of a big coffee can with a lid, I saw a tipped-over can. The lid had come off.

The dirt had spilled out. I could not see a single worm.

There was only one thing to do. It would ruin Daddy's surprise. But that could not be helped. I ran into the living room and told Hannie and Nancy what had happened. Then I got a pan and a wooden spoon from the kitchen. I ran through the house, banging on the pan.

"Worm alert!" I yelled. "Worm alert!"

It did not take long for everyone to wake up. My family and the Daweses and the Papadakises all looked very sleepy as I explained the problem. Then they looked sleepy and grumpy.

"Worms!" groaned Sam. "Oh, no!"

"Only Karen could do something like this," said Charlie.

"We have to look for them," I explained.

"Well, worms cannot travel very fast," said Daddy, scratching his head. (He was still in his pajamas.) "We will try to round them up."

I could not help giggling. The idea of a worm roundup was funny. As if we were cowboys and cowgirls, riding horses and lassoing humongous worms.

Everyone got dressed fast. Even before they were dressed, they started finding worms.

"Karen! There is a worm on the floor in here," called Kristy from the girls' bedroom. I ran in with my can and the spaghetti tongs and scooped it up.

"Karen! Over here!" yelled David Michael. He pointed behind the living room couch. I got that one too.

That is how I spent the next half hour, scooping up worms.

Charlie started laughing. "Those worms must be so confused," he said. He pretended to be a worm, looking around the room. "Where am I? Where am I?"

He and Sam and David Michael fell over laughing.

Finally no one could spot any more

worms. Elizabeth said she would not be surprised if worms kept popping up for years to come.

"Eww," said Mary Anne.

I felt very disappointed. I had wanted to have a special Father's Day gift for Daddy. But my plan had backfired. I handed him the can full of runaway worms. "I am sorry, Daddy. These were for the fishing contest. But instead I just started your day off badly."

Daddy took the can and kissed me. "It was a lovely thought, Karen," he said. "And I still have these nice rounded-up worms for the contest. Thank you."

"You are welcome," I said. "Happy Father's Day."

"Now I have an announcement to make," said Daddy. "I have rented two boats. So we will have three boats altogether for the fishing contest. Mr. Dawes will captain one boat, I will captain one, and Mrs. Papadakis will captain the third. This way we will have

room for everybody who wants to go on a boat."

Hannie and Nancy decided to go on their families' boats. I was a little sad they would not be with me. But the good news was, we now had room for Keegan on our boat! So I was very glad after all.

Let the Contest Begin!

Some people at Shadow Lake take the fishing contest very seriously. But my family and friends and I just wanted to have fun. Daddy took our small boat, the *Faith Pierson*, out to a nice spot on the lake where we would not be too crowded. Mr. Dawes and Mrs. Papadakis steered their boats close to ours. So Hannie and Nancy and I could still see each other and talk to each other.

Keegan had shown up right on time. He was wearing shorts, a T-shirt, and a sun hat. He was carrying his own pole. "It's my father's," he said. He looked as if he were trying to be brave about his daddy's not being here on Father's Day. To cheer him up, I told him my latest joke.

"Knock, knock," I said.

"Who is there?" asked Keegan with a smile.

"Impatient cow," I said.

Keegan's eyebrows sort of scrunched together as he tried to figure out the punchline. But he could not. So he started to say, "Impat —"

"Moo!" I burst in, before he could finish.

We both laughed hard.

I had brought my camera with me, just in case we suddenly saw the Lake Monster. In the meantime, I took lots of pictures of Daddy, Keegan, David Michael, Kristy, and Mary Anne. (Sam and Charlie were fishing off of our dock. Nannie, Elizabeth, and Emily Michelle were keeping them company.)

Hannie and Nancy were taking pictures too. Whenever I saw them pointing a camera in my direction, I smiled hugely.

Daddy was using his Father's Day worms for bait. I could not even bear to watch him put them on the hook. Keegan and I were using stale popcorn for bait.

"Thanks for letting me come, Mr. Brewer," said Keegan.

"We are glad to have you, Keegan," said Daddy.

For just a moment, Keegan looked sad. Then his fishing pole jerked, and his eyes flew wide open. "I have one!" he said.

He quickly turned the handle on his reel and pulled on the pole with all his might. Daddy got ready with the net. On the end of Keegan's line was a nice-sized trout!

"Hooray!" I cried. "The first fish of the day!"

Keegan was very happy. Daddy helped him take the trout off the hook and put it in our ice chest. Then Keegan put another piece of popcorn on his hook and dropped the line back in the water.

I was not catching anything, but I did not

mind *too* much. I had wanted to win a prize for biggest fish or most beautiful fish, but that was not really important. After all, it was a beautiful day. The sun was flashing off the water. Tiny waves lapped the sides of our boat. Hannie and Nancy were calling jokes to Keegan and me. I drank an icy cold root beer. It was a gigundoly great day.

The next person on our boat to catch a fish was David Michael. He caught a bluegill big enough to keep. Into the ice chest it went. After that everyone started catching fish. Daddy, Keegan, David Michael, Kristy, Mary Anne — they all caught fish. Our ice chest was full of trout and bluegills and even some bass. I was the only person who was not catching fish. But maybe it was because I was talking and laughing and snapping pictures and taking a poll to see who was using what bait. I was starting to think that maybe fish are vegetarians, but they had been eating Daddy's worms, so . . .

Keegan was telling me another knock-knock joke when I realized my pole was being tugged gently. I sat up quickly and clutched my pole tighter. I pulled harder and harder.

"I have something!" I yelled. "I have something!"

Mary Anne got the net ready, but I could not pull up the fish. "It is too heavy!" I said to Daddy. "Help!"

Daddy held my pole too and helped me pull.

"Gee, this fish must be *really* big," said Daddy. He pulled even harder.

"Do not let him get away," I said. I held on to the pole and pulled as hard as I could. Suddenly my line popped out of the water. At the end of the line was a big brown . . . baseball glove.

I stared at it. It hung from my line, dripping water. It was a yucky old baseball glove that looked as if it had been sitting on the bottom of the lake since before baseball was invented.

David Michael was the first one to laugh. He pointed at it and doubled over.

"I am sorry, Karen," said Daddy. "I thought you had a really big fish." I could tell he was trying not to smile. For a moment I felt very disappointed. I had been practicing fishing all week, and I had not caught a single fish. Now everyone around me was catching fish (even Hannie and Nancy). My own little sister had caught a fish with a *pretend* fishing pole. And what had I caught?

A baseball glove.

I could not help it. I stared at the dripping glove, and saw that everyone was trying not to laugh (except David Michael). Then I started to laugh too. It seemed so funny. It was the funniest thing that had ever happened to me. I could not *stop* laughing.

So everyone else gave in. Daddy laughed until tears ran out of his eyes. I opened the ice chest and put my glove in on top of everyone's fish. Mary Anne and Kristy began laughing so hard they had to sit down.

Keegan could not even hold his fishing pole. I grabbed my camera and took pictures of everyone. Daddy borrowed my camera and took a picture of me holding up my glove.

It was a great fishing trip.

Good-bye, Shadow Lake

Guess what. I won a prize in the Shadow Lake fishing contest after all. I won the "Most Original Fish" award. Keegan won the "Biggest Fish Caught by Someone Twelve or Under" award. I was gigundoly glad he had won something. He looked completely happy by the end of the day.

"I am the only person who caught any bass," said Daddy smugly as we walked back to the house. He put an arm around me. "It is because I was using Karen's special worms."

That made me feel good.

That night the grown-ups cleaned the fish and we had a great fish cookout. Besides delicious fish, we ate corn on the cob, fresh green beans, baked potatoes, corn bread, and peach cobbler. Yum, yum, yum. I asked for seconds of everything.

The very next morning it was time to pack up and go back to Stoneybrook. We were sad to leave, but our mommies and daddies had to get back to work. First Nannie took off in the Pink Clinker with Emily Michelle and Elizabeth and Kristy and Mary Anne. Then Mr. and Mrs. Dawes drove off with Danny. Then Charlie drove away in Elizabeth's car with Sam and David Michael and Linny Papadakis. Then the Papadakises left with Sari. Finally it was just the Three Musketeers and Daddy.

We were loading the last suitcase into the car when Keegan came running down our driveway.

"I just wanted to say good-bye," he said,

panting. "And to thank you again for the fishing contest."

"I am so glad we got to see you this week," I said.

"Me too," said Hannie.

"Me three," said Nancy. My friends liked Keegan, which made me happy.

"We will write and tell you the next time we are coming to Shadow Lake," I said. "Then maybe you and your mom can come then too."

"Yeah," said Keegan.

Hannie and Nancy got in the car. I leaned over to Keegan.

"Try not to worry about your parents too much," I whispered. "Getting a divorce is very hard. But your mommy and daddy still both love you. Do not forget that."

"Okay," whispered Keegan. "Thank you."

Then I hopped in the car, fastened my seat belt, and we were on our way home.

"Can you come over?" I said into the phone. "Nancy is on her way. I just got all my pictures back from Shadow Lake!"

"I will be right over," said Hannie.

One whole week had gone by since our fishing trip to Shadow Lake. Usually Hannie and Nancy and I played together every day. Not always, though. Sometimes even best friends need a little break.

But today I had five packages of photographs to show them. I had not even opened them myself yet. I had a brand-new photo album all ready to put pictures in.

Ten minutes later the Three Musketeers were sitting in my room at the big house.

"I have to choose a stack of pictures to send to Mommy and Andrew and Seth," I said. "And a stack for the album. And some for Keegan and —"

"Open them up!" said Hannie. "Let us see."

My pictures were mostly wonderful. A few were bad, because I had cut off someone's head or feet. A couple were too dark or were out of focus. But there were a lot of great ones.

"Oh my gosh, here we are in our monster-watching shelter," said Nancy. "In the rain!"

"Here we are making clover chains on the lawn," said Hannie.

"This is the one that Kristy took of us," I said. "I will have two copies made, one for each of you."

"Thank you," said Hannie. "Oh, look, this is the fishing contest. Here is the one your daddy took, of your most original fish."

Hannie and Nancy started laughing all over again. The picture showed me standing proudly in Daddy's boat. I was holding up my line, with the soggy glove attached. It was a really funny picture.

"What is that, in the water?" I asked when I had stopped laughing. I pointed to a dark spot in the background of the picture. "Is that the shadow of a cloud?"

Hannie peered at it. "No." She shook her head. "It is too small for a cloud."

"Maybe it is the shadow of a plane overhead," I said.

"Maybe," said Hannie. "I guess it could be."

Nancy's eyes grew big. "You guys," she said. "Maybe it is not a shadow from *above*, but a shadow from *below*."

I shook my head. "No," I said. "It is too big. No fish is that —"

I stared at Hannie and Nancy. They stared back at me.

"The Lake Monster!" we all yelled at the same time.

We showed the picture to everyone we knew. No one could say that it was *not* the Lake Monster. And no one could think of what else it could be. It was a dark, ripply shadow on the lake, with nothing there to make the shadow. Unless something was under the water.

We mailed a copy of the picture to Keegan right away.

"Next time he can monster-watch in our shelter with us," said Nancy.

"We will need a bigger shelter," said Hannie. "A rainproof one."

"And we will need more film," I said.

We started planning our next trip to Shadow Lake.

And you know what? It looked as if I had caught the biggest fish after all! On film!

L. GODWIN

About the Author

ANN M. MARTIN lives in New York City and loves animals, especially cats. She has two cats of her own, Gussie and Woody.

Other books by Ann M. Martin that you might enjoy are *Stage Fright*; *Me and Katie (the Pest)*; and the books in *The Baby-sitters Club* series.

Ann likes ice cream and *I Love Lucy*. And she has her own little sister, whose name is Jane.

Little Sister

Don't miss #99

KAREN'S BIG CITY MYSTERY

Mommy turned back to me. (I had let Rocky go. He was eating a snack under the kitchen sink.) "It is not a fire," she said. "It is a burglar alarm. There has been a robbery in the building."

I gasped. "You are kidding! Where?"

"I am not sure," said Mommy. "But the police are on their way."

I headed for the front door. "I have to go ask Donald what happened," I said.

"Wait, please, Karen," said Mommy. "I would like you to stay in our apartment while the police are trying to do their job. We do not know where the burglar is or what happened." She went and double-locked the front door. A shiver went down my spine.

BABY-SITTERS

Little Sister

by Ann M. Martin,
author of The Baby-sitters Club ®

More Titles... ➡

The Baby-sitters Little Sister titles continued...

❑	MQ48306-4	#61	Karen's Tattletale	$2.95
❑	MQ48307-2	#62	Karen's New Bike	$2.95
❑	MQ25996-2	#63	Karen's Movie	$2.95
❑	MQ25997-0	#64	Karen's Lemonade Stand	$2.95
❑	MQ25998-9	#65	Karen's Toys	$2.95
❑	MQ26279-3	#66	Karen's Monsters	$2.95
❑	MQ26024-3	#67	Karen's Turkey Day	$2.95
❑	MQ26025-1	#68	Karen's Angel	$2.95
❑	MQ26193-2	#69	Karen's Big Sister	$2.95
❑	MQ26280-7	#70	Karen's Grandad	$2.95
❑	MQ26194-0	#71	Karen's Island Adventure	$2.95
❑	MQ26195-9	#72	Karen's New Puppy	$2.95
❑	MQ26301-3	#73	Karen's Dinosaur	$2.95
❑	MQ26214-9	#74	Karen's Softball Mystery	$2.95
❑	MQ69183-X	#75	Karen's County Fair	$2.95
❑	MQ69184-8	#76	Karen's Magic Garden	$2.95
❑	MQ69185-6	#77	Karen's School Surprise	$2.99
❑	MQ69186-4	#78	Karen's Half Birthday	$2.99
❑	MQ69187-2	#79	Karen's Big Fight	$2.99
❑	MQ69188-0	#80	Karen's Christmas Tree	$2.99
❑	MQ69189-9	#81	Karen's Accident	$2.99
❑	MQ69190-2	#82	Karen's Secret Valentine	$3.50
❑	MQ69191-0	#83	Karen's Bunny	$3.50
❑	MQ69192-9	#84	Karen's Big Job	$3.50
❑	MQ69193-7	#85	Karen's Treasure	$3.50
❑	MQ69194-5	#86	Karen's Telephone Trouble	$3.50
❑	MQ06585-8	#87	Karen's Pony Camp	$3.50
❑	MQ06586-6	#88	Karen's Puppet Show	$3.50
❑	MQ06587-4	#89	Karen's Unicorn	$3.50
❑	MQ06588-2	#90	Karen's Haunted House	$3.50
❑	MQ06589-0	#91	Karen's Pilgrim	$3.50
❑	MQ06590-4	#92	Karen's Sleigh Ride	$3.50
❑	MQ06591-2	#93	Karen's Cooking Contest	$3.50
❑	MQ06592-0	#94	Karen's Snow Princess	$3.50
❑	MQ06593-9	#95	Karen's Promise	$3.50
❑	MQ06594-7	#96	Karen's Big Move	$3.50
❑	MQ06595-5	#97	Karen's Paper Route	$3.50
❑	MQ55407-7		BSLS Jump Rope Pack	$5.99
❑	MQ73914-X		BSLS Playground Games Pack	$5.99
❑	MQ89735-7		BSLS Photo Scrapbook Book and Camera Pack	$9.99
❑	MQ47677-7		BSLS School Scrapbook	$2.95
❑	MQ43647-3		Karen's Wish Super Special #1	$3.25
❑	MQ44834-X		Karen's Plane Trip Super Special #2	$3.25
❑	MQ44827-7		Karen's Mystery Super Special #3	$3.25
❑	MQ45644-X		Karen, Hannie, and Nancy The Three Musketeers Super Special #4	$2.95
❑	MQ45649-0		Karen's Baby Super Special #5	$3.50
❑	MQ46911-8		Karen's Campout Super Special #6	$3.25

Available wherever you buy books, or use this order form.

Scholastic Inc., P.O. Box 7502, 2931 E. McCarty Street, Jefferson City, MO 65102

Please send me the books I have checked above. I am enclosing $_____
(please add $2.00 to cover shipping and handling). Send check or money order – no
cash or C.O.Ds please.

Name_____ Birthdate _____

Address_____

City_____ State/Zip _____